Magic Ponies

Circus Surprise

To Ginger, plucky brave little friend—SB

GROSSET & DUNLAP
Published by the Penguin Group
Penguin Group (USA) LLC, 375 Hudson Street, New York, New York 10014, USA

USA | Canada | UK | Ireland | Australia | New Zealand | India | South Africa | China

penguin.com
A Penguin Random House Company

Text copyright © 2009 by Sue Bentley. Illustrations copyright © 2009 by Angela Swan. Cover illustration © 2009 by Andrew Farley. First printed as *Seaside Summer* in Great Britain in 2009 by Penguin Books Ltd. First published in the United States in 2014 by Grosset & Dunlap, a division of Penguin Young Readers Group, 345 Hudson Street, New York, New York 10014. GROSSET & DUNLAP is a trademark of Penguin Group (USA) LLC. Printed in the USA.

Library of Congress Cataloging-in-Publication Data is available.

ISBN 978-0-448-46734-4   10 9 8 7 6 5 4 3 2 1

Circus Surprise

SUE BENTLEY

illustrated by Angela Swan

Grosset & Dunlap
An Imprint of Penguin Group (USA) LLC

Prologue

The young magic pony folded his gold-feathered wings as he soared down toward Rainbow Mist Island. Moments later, Comet's hooves landed on a stretch of shining pebble beach. It felt good to be home.

His tummy felt full of butterflies as he wondered if Destiny had found her way home at last. Comet's twin sister had been

lost for so long. He was looking forward
to finding her safe among their family of
Lightning Horses.

Tossing his head so that his golden
mane fell forward onto his cream neck,
the magic pony trotted away from the sea
and headed up the steep hillside.

He reached the top and stood looking
down toward the familiar rolling plains
and forests. In the distance were the
mountains, wreathed in the shimmering
multicolored mist that gave the island its
name.

A warm breeze rippled through the
silvery grass, bringing the scent of fresh
water toward the magic pony. Comet's
deep violet eyes gleamed, and he snorted
as he galloped down a slope.

Sunlight flashed on his smooth pale-

cream coat and golden silky mane and tail.
He reached the spring that trickled over
some stones into a small pool and bent his
head for a drink.

A movement flickered over the nearby
rocks, and Comet saw the shadow of a
large horse in the rippling water.

The magic pony threw up his head,
his eyes wide in alarm. Was this another
Lightning Horse or one of the dark horses
who wanted to steal his magic? His pulse
quickened as he slowly turned around.

An older horse with a wise expression
and kind dark eyes stepped into view.
"Blaze!" Comet bent his head before the
leader of the Lightning Herd.

"I am glad to see you again, Comet,"
Blaze said warmly, in a deep velvety neigh.
"Is Destiny with you?"

Comet felt a pang of disappointment. "No. I thought she must have found her way back safely by now."

"I am afraid not. I do not think Destiny will return while she believes herself to be in terrible trouble for losing the Stone of Power," Blaze told him.

The Stone of Power protected the Lightning Herd from the dark horses. Destiny had accidentally lost it when she and Comet were playing their favorite game, cloud-racing. Comet had found the stone, but Destiny had already fled.

"I wish I knew where Destiny was hiding." Comet's proud, arching neck drooped sadly.

"The stone will help us to find her." Blaze pawed at the ground with one shining hoof. A fire opal, glinting with

many colors, appeared. As Comet and
Blaze looked deeply into it, the stone
grew larger and an image appeared in its
shimmering depths.

Comet saw his twin sister galloping
along the sandy shore of a place in a far-
off world. "Destiny!"

"She is alone and in danger," Blaze
said. "You must go and find her before the
dark horses discover where she is!"

There was a flash of bright violet
light and a rainbow mist appeared around
Comet. The light-cream pony with golden
wings disappeared, and in his place stood a
handsome pony with a white coat covered
with black spots, a white mane and tail,
and large deep violet eyes.

Comet snorted. "I will use this disguise
to search for Destiny!"

"Go now," urged Blaze, nodding. "There is no time to lose. Bring her back safely!"

"I will!" Comet vowed.

He neighed softly as violet sparkles ignited in his spotted coat and he felt the power building inside him. The rainbow mist swirled more thickly, twinkling as it drew Comet in.

Chapter ONE

"Bye, thanks for visiting! Hope we'll see you again soon," Jessie Starkling called politely as the last few kids and grown-ups climbed down from the carousel horses and wandered away across the fairground.

"That's the way, Jess. Number one rule: Always leave the customers happy. That way, they're sure to come back," her dad said, smiling.

Jess smiled back at him. It had been
a long day helping out on the merry-go-
round, and she was hot and tired. Tossing
back her braid of glossy dark hair, she
began flipping the controls that shut
off the merry-go-round's hundreds of
lights.

Her dad was already counting the
day's earnings. He was the youngest of

the three brothers who owned and ran the Starkling Brothers' Circus.

"One day you'll be running the fair, looking after all the rides, just like me," Mr. Starkling said to his daughter.

"Yeah! In about a million years!" Jess's fourteen-year-old cousin, Mai, teased. She was tall with the same chocolate-brown eyes and glossy dark hair as Jess, but Mai's was shoulder length with bangs. Her dad was the oldest of the Starkling brothers. She often lent an extra hand with the merry-go-round at the busiest times on the fairground.

"Says you! I might only be nine, but everyone knows kids grow up quickly in the circus!" Jess countered, her eyes sparkling.

Her dad nodded agreement. "You certainly know all there is to know about this beauty," he said, making a sweeping gesture with both arms at the beautiful merry-go-round.

Jess felt a surge of pride. She loved the carousel, which was well over a hundred years old. It had a double row of twenty-four galloping horses, and each part of it was covered with gilded carvings and tiny sparkling mirrors.

Jess adored every single one of the beautiful painted and gilded horses. She didn't mind all the work it took to keep them shiny and bright. But she also had a secret that not even Mai knew about.

Her dearest wish in the whole world was to have a real pony of her own.

Jess swallowed a sigh as she unlocked a compartment in the central pillar and reached for the night covers to put on

the rides. What was the point of wanting
what you couldn't have? The only horses
allowed on-site were those in the bareback
act, which was performed in the big top.

"Penny for your thoughts?" Mai said.
"You've got that glassy-eyed look again.
What are you thinking about?"

"Oh, nothing much," Jess said
evasively.

Her dad was locking the cash box.
"I'm going to run now," he told the girls.
"There's a meeting in the big top, after the
evening performance. See you both later."

"Okay," Jess said. She was used to
shutting the ride down for the night and
could do it with her eyes closed. "Do you
know what the meeting's about?" she
asked her cousin as her dad walked away.

Mai shrugged. "Probably about the

new site for next summer. It's all anyone's talking about."

Jess nodded. The news was all anyone was talking about around the circus. The site at Treen-&-Sea, which had been the summer home of the Starkling Brothers' Circus for the last thirty-five years, was being sold so a new housing devlopment could be built on it. It had been a major shock to everyone, including Jess.

"Why don't you go and find out

what's going on?" she suggested to her cousin.

"I'll finish up here and then follow you."

Mai looked tempted, but she hesitated. "Sure you'll be okay by yourself?"

Jess widened her brown eyes and gave her cousin an "are you kidding?" look. She was related to virtually every person around here. There was nowhere on earth where she was safer!

Mai laughed and gave in. "All right then. Thanks, Jess. You're a star!"

As soon as she was alone, Jess picked up a soft cloth and began happily wiping down the carousel horses. She did this every night, even when the horses didn't need it. They were all so handsome, with their different-colored manes and tails and brightly painted saddles.

But one of them was Jess's special favorite. It was a prancing white horse with black spots all over it like a Dalmatian. It had pricked ears, a particularly sweet face with realistic glass eyes, and blue-and-green trimmings with gold highlights.

Jess ran her hand over the high-arched wooden neck and flowing mane and tail. A stir of longing swept through her as she wished she could have a pony just like this one. On impulse she mounted it and then put her feet in the stirrups. Reaching forward, she patted the glossy wooden neck.

"Well, horsey. How would you like to go for a midnight ride? Just you and me,"

she said softly, laughing at the very idea.

Suddenly there was a bright violet flash, and a thick glittering rainbow mist sparkling in the lights of the fairground.

"Oh!" She blinked, trying to see through the strange mist.

As it slowly cleared, Jess felt a tremor beneath her palm and the carousel horse shook its head. Swishing its tail, it straightened its legs and placed its four shining hooves firmly on the wooden platform.

"Hold tight, please!" it said in a velvety neigh.

Chapter
TWO

Jess almost fell off sideways in shock.
What was happening? She must be so tired
out after the busy evening that she was
imagining things! Carousel horses didn't
move, and they certainly couldn't speak.

Before she had time to gather her
thoughts, the pony sprang forward in a mighty
leap. He cleared the carousel horse in front
and landed a few feet away on the grass.

"Oh!" Jess gasped, clinging on with trembling fingers.

Somehow she kept her balance by sitting down firmly in the saddle and gripping the horse's sides tightly with her legs. She wrapped her hands in the spotted pony's thick, flowing white mane as it galloped across the fairground, weaving between the other rides and stalls in a dizzying burst of speed.

There was a strange tingling feeling
flowing to the ends of Jess's fingers, and
bright violet sparks glinted in the pony's
spotted coat. It was weird, but she felt safe,
however fast they were going. In no time at
all, they reached the edge of the fairground
and came to a halt behind the big Tilt-A-
Whirl, which was dark and closed up for
the night.

"Please get down now," the pony
whinnied gently.

Jess did so, still having trouble taking it
all in. The moment her feet touched the
ground, her legs started shaking and she
almost sank to her knees.

The spotted pony quickly positioned
itself so that she could lean against its strong
shoulder. As Jess touched the warm silky
skin, she felt herself starting to calm down.

"I am sorry if I frightened you," the spotted pony whinnied apologetically. "My name is Comet of the Lightning Herd. What is your name?"

Jess blinked at him. The amazing pony was breathing warm air through his nostrils in a friendly manner. To her surprise, she saw that he had glowing deep violet eyes.

"I'm J-J-Jessie. Jessie S-S-Starkling," she stammered. "But everyone calls me Jess. My dad and his two brothers own this circus."

The pony bent his neck in a formal bow. "I am honored to meet you, Jess."

"Um . . . me too." Jess's curiosity was working overtime. "I don't get it. What just happened? One minute you were a carousel horse, and now you're real and you can talk! That's never happened before."

"All of the Lightning Herd can talk. I live with them on Rainbow Mist Island, but I have come here to search for my twin sister, Destiny. I saw the moving machine with all the wooden horses and it seemed like a good place to hide. When you climbed onto my back, you took me by surprise."

Jess grinned. "Tell me about it! I think we *both* had quite a shock!"

Comet tossed his head in agreement, his bright eyes sparkling with amusement.

"Is Destiny one of the carousel horses, too?" Jess wanted to know.

"No. She is lost somewhere nearby in this world."

Jess nodded slowly. "But why did Destiny come here in the first place?"

Concern flickered across Comet's spotted face. "My twin sister thinks she is responsible for losing the Stone of Power that protects our herd from our enemies," he explained. "She lost it during one of our games of cloud-racing. I found the stone, but Destiny thought she was in terrible trouble and already had fled. Now she is in danger from the dark horses who would like to steal her magic."

Jess listened closely. It all sounded so strange and wonderful. One thing in particular puzzled her. "Cloud-racing? How . . . ?"

Comet backed away slowly. "Please stay there," he ordered.

Jess felt another warm prickling sensation flow to the tips of her fingers as violet-colored sparkles bloomed in Comet's white-and-black coat and more of the glittering rainbow mist rippled round him. The handsome spotted pony disappeared and in its place stood a majestic cream-colored pony with a proudly arched neck and a flowing golden mane and tail. Springing from his shoulders were magnificent wings, covered with glowing bright golden feathers.

Jess was totally speechless. She had never seen anything so beautiful in her whole life.

"Comet? Is . . . is that still you?" she gulped when she found her voice again.

"Yes, Jess. This is my true form. Do not be afraid." Comet gave a soft, musical whinny. There was a final swirl of the magical sparkling mist and Comet instantly reappeared as a white-and-black spotted pony with a white mane and tail.

"Wow! That's a great disguise. Is Destiny hiding as a normal pony, too?" Jess asked.

"Yes. She will also be in disguise, but that will not save her if the dark horses discover her," Comet told her seriously. "I must start looking for her. Will you help me?"

Jess saw that his beautiful, deep violet eyes were shadowed by sadness. *He must be missing his twin sister.* Her heart went out to the lonely magic pony.

"Of course I'll help you. We'll search for Destiny together!"

"Thank you, Jess." Comet stepped forward and pushed his satiny nose into her cupped hands.

Jess stroked him, totally charmed. "I can't wait to tell Mai about this. She's my older cousin and thinks she's really grown up, but she's—"

"No!" Comet lifted his head. "I am sorry, Jess, but you can't tell anyone about me or what I have told you."

Jess was disappointed that she couldn't even tell Mai. It would have been great to share such a wonderful secret with her cousin.

"You must promise," Comet neighed seriously, looking into her face with his intelligent eyes.

Jess nodded slowly. If it would help
protect his twin sister from the dark
horses until Comet could find her, she was
prepared to keep his secret. She knew how
she would feel if Mai was the one missing.
"Okay. I promise. Cross my heart."

"Thank you, Jess."

Jess smiled at him and reached up
to pat his satiny spotted cheek. She had
another thought. "Where are you going to
stay? The only ponies allowed on the site
are those that perform in the circus."

Comet tossed his head. "I will hide as
a carousel horse again."

"But . . . how's that going to work?"
Jess asked. "Customers will want to ride
on you when the merry-go-round's
working. Won't it be difficult for you to
stay really still all the time?"

"I do not mind if people ride me on the big machine. It will be fun," Comet told her, swishing his flowing tail. "And I will use my magic, so that only you will see and hear me. Everyone else will just see a carved wooden horse."

"Cool!" Jess exclaimed. "The circus and fairground are closed during the day on weekdays, so we'll have a lot of time to go out looking for Destiny together."

Comet nodded, his eyes lighting up at the thought of finding his twin sister.

"We'd better go back now, before someone notices that one of the carousel horses is missing," Jess pointed out. "Besides, Mai will be wondering why I'm taking so long to close up for the night."

"Very well. Climb onto my back again," Comet said.

Jess felt a wave of excitement as
she climbed up onto Comet's back and
wrapped her hands in his mane. There was
a final flash of violet light, visible only to
Jess, as Comet shot forward. In no time at
all, she was sitting on the merry-go-round,
riding what appeared to be a normal
spotted carousel horse.

"See you later!" she whispered as she gave Comet a hug before carefully sliding down and putting the canvas cover over him.

She only just managed to stop herself from laughing out loud with happiness. Her dream of having a pony of her own had come true! But in a way she could never have imagined—not even in her wildest dreams!

Chapter
THREE

"I can't believe that Uncle Felix wants
to leave the circus!" Mai exclaimed, as
she poked her head in through the open
trailer door early the following morning.
"How can he even think of staying put
somewhere and getting a normal job?"

Jess was just sitting down to eat her
breakfast. She'd had an amazing dream
about flying through the air on Comet.

It had felt so real, even down to the
softness of his warm gold-feathered wings
brushing against her. The wonderful
images still filled her mind.

"Um . . . yeah. That's too awful
to think about." Jess forced herself to
concentrate on what her cousin was
saying. "Maybe Uncle Felix didn't mean it,
about leaving."

Jess's mom smiled at Mai. "Come on
in. You can't talk about this stuff on an
empty stomach. We're having scrambled
eggs. There's plenty for one extra."

Mai smiled despite herself. "Thanks, Aunt Lily." Still looking worried, Mai took a plate from her aunt and sat down next to Jess.

"So how come you took so long putting everything away last night, anyway?" Mai asked, chewing thoughtfully. "You were there forever."

Jess looked surprised at her cousin. There had been so many people in the big top, all talking at once, that she hadn't realized Mai had noticed that she was late. "I . . . um, was chatting with . . . someone," she replied vaguely. *You wouldn't believe who it was, even if I could tell you!* she thought. "What did they say at the meeting?"

"Well." Her mom spoke first. "New houses are going up everywhere. There's not much open land left. I'm afraid that your dad thinks Felix has a point."

Jess realized with a little jolt of dismay that her mom looked really worried. This was serious. Surely her dad wouldn't leave the circus!

She looked at Mai. "What does Uncle Oliver say?" she asked her cousin.

"Dad's dead set against quitting. He says the circus is in our blood! I'm with him. The Starklings have been circus people for generations. I'd rather die than do anything else!" she said fiercely.

Jess pushed her scrambled eggs around with a fork. Mai was always so dramatic, but this time Jess agreed with her. She couldn't think of anything worse than living in a normal house in a dull town, instead of traveling to the coast every summer and spending the season there.

They finished eating in silence.
Mai thanked her aunt for the food and
then she and Jess helped clear away
the dishes before they went off to do
their chores.

"I'm collecting trash today. Bor–ing!"
Mai said, rolling her eyes. "At least I can
listen to music while I do it. See you
later!" She put on her headphones as she
wandered away.

Jess waved to her and then made her
way to the temporary stables, where the
troop of six handsome circus horses lived
during the season. One of them, Samson,
a large gray, leaned his head over his stall
and nudged at her pocket for the treats
she usually brought him.

"Hey! Stop that, Samson!" Jess said,
laughing, fishing out a mint for him.

She helped with mucking out the
stalls and then changed water buckets and
filled hay nets. Usually she felt a twinge of
sadness, desperately longing for a pony of
her own.

But today she was in high spirits. She
might not yet *own* her own pony, but now

she had a gorgeous, secret magic pony to keep her company.

As soon as she'd finished, Jess hurried toward the merry-go-round. Quickly checking that no one was looking, she lifted Comet's cover and stowed it away out of sight.

Comet gave a whicker of welcome as he shook himself. "Hello, Jess!"

Jess stroked his silky spotted neck delightedly. "Hi, Comet. We can go for a ride together now to see if we can find Destiny. I think we have a few hours before anyone wonders where I am."

Luckily, Comet was one of the inner-ring horses, so someone would have to look really closely to notice that one carousel horse was missing.

"Thank you, Jess. Climb onto my back."

"But what if someone sees us?" she asked worriedly.

"I will use my magic so no one will see either of us while you are riding me." Comet pawed at the wooden boards with one front hoof.

Jess climbed onto his back and almost immediately she felt a familiar tingling in her fingertips as Comet's spotted coat twinkled with violet sparks and a faint rainbow mist swirled around them.

"Ready?" Comet neighed.

"Definitely!"

"Hold on tight!" Comet rocked back onto his hind legs and pawed the air before soaring over the other carousel horses in such a huge leap that it felt as if they were flying.

Jess caught her breath with excitement
as they sped away. It was thrilling to ride
Comet, who was so smooth and fast. His
hooves hardly seemed to touch the ground
as he raced onward at the speed of light.

Jess crouched low on his back, moving in time to his powerful strides. She had never ridden a pony flat out before, but she didn't feel even a little bit afraid. Shining rainbows gleamed in Comet's flowing white mane as his magic spread over her, making her feel warm and safe.

Soon the circus and fairground were far behind them. Jess told Comet that it would be safe for them both to become visible now, as they were not likely to meet anyone she knew. The magic pony nodded, and in a flash of sparkly violet magic it was done.

Jess pointed him toward a quiet narrow road, lined on both sides with wild-rose hedges. Their sweet scent filled the air as they swept past. "This leads to the beach and the cliff tops. From up there we'll be able to see for miles."

Comet galloped on tirelessly. As the
beach came into sight, he gradually slowed
to a trot and then a walk.

They began crossing a short stretch of
soft sand. The magic pony's head turned
from side to side as his keen eyes searched
for signs of Destiny. Jess kept a lookout,
too, but they saw no other ponies.

It was still early, and the sun wasn't
yet hot. One or two people were walking
dogs, and a few families with kids were
building sandcastles. Jess knew that later
on, this quiet beach would be filled with
people relaxing on their vacations.

Near the shore, there was a long
stretch of solid wet sand. The breakers
came in with a shushing noise and cool
white foam swirled around Comet's legs

as he high-stepped along. With a neigh
of pleasure he sped up, kicking up spray
behind him as they rode on under a
cloudless blue sky.

Jess felt a glow of perfect happiness
spread through her chest. This had to
be the best thing ever—riding the most
amazing pony in the universe through the
shallow waves on a perfect day! She knew
she'd never forget it.

"The beach stretches on forever. There are hundreds of caves in these cliffs, and miles and miles of rough land on the cliff tops. How will we find Destiny?" she asked Comet.

The spotted pony twitched his silky white tail. "We have a special bond because we are twins. If Destiny is close, I will sense her presence. Also, wherever she goes she will leave a trail."

"A trail? What will it look like?" Jess asked.

"There will be softly glowing hoofprints, which are invisible to most people in this world."

"Wow!" Jess said, fascinated. "Will I be able to see them?"

"Yes. If you are riding me or I am very close to you," Comet told her. A flicker of excitement passed over his spotted skin, and he stretched his neck to peer up the beach, where a line of ponies were just emerging from a path down the hill.

Jess had seen them, too. "Do you think that one of those ponies might be Destiny? Let's go and see!"

Chapter FOUR

Jess rose to a trot as Comet's hooves drummed on the packed sand and he closed the distance between himself and the other ponies.

She could see now that there were five of them. Four were being ridden by small children, with an older girl on a stocky chestnut mare leading the group. She smiled and waved when she saw Jess approaching.

Jess felt encouraged by the girl's
friendly expression. "Hi! It's a great day for
riding, isn't it?" she called out, as she and
Comet reached the riders.

"Yeah! Just perfect," the girl said,
slowing her chestnut mare. Behind her,
the young riders reined in their ponies.
"Take five, everyone. We'll give the ponies
a short rest," she said to them with a smile.

Comet whinnied and gave a friendly
snort as he looked closely at the five
ponies. They, in turn, tossed their heads
and flicked their ears forward. One or two

nickered back, and Jess's heart leaped with hope for her magical friend.

But Comet turned away, his head drooping. None of them was Destiny. Jess realized that it wasn't going to be so simple to find her. She could tell that her magic pony was worried about his twin sister, who was lost and all alone.

"We'll keep searching. And we won't stop until we find Destiny," she promised him in a whisper, patting his silky neck.

"Thank you, Jess," Comet neighed softly.

The girl on the chestnut mare looked at Jess curiously. "I'm Ellen. Ellen Bridgemore." She looked about twelve years old and had short fair hair and a round, pretty face. "I often bring rides down onto the beach, but I haven't seen you around here before."

"Um . . . no. I just got Comet," Jess said. It wasn't exactly a lie, because Comet *had* only just chosen her to be his friend. "It's the first time I've been out on a long ride with him. I'm Jessie Starkling, by the way. But everyone calls me Jess."

"Wow! Your first real ride together? That's exciting for you both," Ellen enthused. "It's so much fun working with a new pony and getting to know him, isn't it? Comet's gorgeous. Such unusual spotted markings."

"Yes. Comet's *very* unusual, all right," Jess said, biting back a grin. She wondered what Ellen would have said if she knew how special Comet really was! "Your pony's beautiful, too. What's her name?" she asked.

Ellen's chestnut pony had a glossy coat. Its face was slightly dished, with a gentle expression and large dark eyes.

"Bliss," Ellen told her. "She's my favorite, although I love all our ponies. Bliss is so steady and good-natured. She'd lead the ride back home even if I fell asleep in the saddle! My mom owns a riding stable in Lower Treen," she explained.

"Really?" Jess said. "It must be hard work taking care of all those ponies."

Ellen nodded. "You bet. But we're not as busy as we used to be." A shadow of worry flickered across her face. "A brand-new riding stable has just opened up down the coast, and some of our customers have started going there. There's only Mom and me, so I usually help out after school and on weekends and vacations, like now. There's nothing else I'd

rather be doing. Ponies rule, right? That's
what I always say—" She stopped as she
seemed to realize that Jess couldn't get a
word in at all. "Sorry!" she said, grinning.
"Once I get started about ponies and
riding, I can go on all day. Mom says she's
going to get me a 'pause' button!"

"That's okay. I like it," Jess said, grinning. "Pony talk is my favorite thing! But I don't know anyone who's as crazy about ponies as I am!"

"You do now!" Ellen joked.

They both laughed.

Jess was enjoying herself. She hoped that she and Ellen might get to know each other better. It was great having Comet as her secret friend, but she couldn't ever let anyone at the circus see him or tell them how wonderful he was. It would be really fun to have a brand-new horse friend to go riding with.

"I've always loved everything about ponies and horses," Jess told Ellen.

"I've wanted one of my own for ages . . . and then Comet suddenly appeared . . . um, I mean, came along," she

corrected quickly. "Before I got him,
I never went for any long rides. I help
take care of the circus horses, so I'm
allowed to ride one of them sometimes,
but only on-site."

Ellen's eyes widened. "Circus . . .?
Oh, you're Jess *Starkling*! I thought I
recognized the name. So your family *owns*
the circus. Mom and Dad took me to see
a show there once. Wow! That's so cool.
It must be an exciting life."

Jess felt herself blushing. She shrugged.
"I guess so. I'm used to it."

Ellen suddenly noticed that the
young riders with her were fidgeting
impatiently. She gave them an apologetic
grin. "Sorry, guys. You didn't come on
a ride to hear me blabber! Why don't
you go down to the shore? You can ride

along in the shallows. But don't go any
faster than a trot and turn back when
you get to the Needle, okay?" she said,
pointing to a tall rock formation that was
visible in the near distance.

"Can I lead, Jess?" a brown-haired
boy on a stout little bay pony piped up
eagerly.

Ellen nodded. "Fine with me, Ross.
You're a confident rider, and you're used
to Sparky."

Ross squared his shoulders and sat up straight. "Follow me, everyone!" he said proudly, urging his pony forward. The others followed, heading down to the patch of packed wet sand and the rolling breakers.

"Ellen's nice, isn't she?" Jess whispered to Comet, while the older girl was distracted. "Do you mind if I stay and chat with her for a while?"

"I would like that. Bliss is a fine pony, too," he whinnied good-naturedly.

"Thanks, Comet. You're the best!" Jess said, feeling a surge of affection for him.

After the young riders had bounced away on their ponies, Ellen turned back to Jess. "So—tell me what it's like to live in a circus. And don't leave anything out!" she joked.

Jess grinned. "This could take a *really* long time!"

While Jess and Ellen chatted, Comet and Bliss breathed in each other's scent and then gently touched noses, making friends in their own pony way.

Deep in conversation, the girls hardly noticed the next few minutes passing, but eventually Ellen checked her watch.

"I'd better go and meet those kids and head back to the stables with them. Their parents will soon be back at the yard waiting to pick them up. Mom doesn't like to keep people waiting. She says it's bad for business."

Jess nodded. She knew all about keeping customers happy.

Ellen narrowed her eyes to peer at the shoreline in the distance. "Here's Ross leading them back now," she said, raising her arm to wave.

Suddenly warning shouts rang out, and a child's bright–orange boat came careening down to the shore. One of the ponies reared in fright and leaped forward into the waves.

"Oh my goodness!" Jess gasped, as the young rider screamed and held on tightly as her pony continued to kick and rear.

"Oh no! That's Lana on Pie!" Ellen cried. "She's one of our newest riders!" Nudging Bliss on, she shot toward the commotion.

Jess already was racing after her on Comet, his white mane and tail streaming out behind him.

At the shore, Ross had brought his pony to a stop. "Ellen! It wasn't my fault.

That boat scared Pie. Now Lana can't get him to come back in." The boy gulped, close to tears.

"It's okay, Ross. I saw what happened. I'll get Pie. The rest of you stay here," Ellen ordered. "The water gets deeper just a few feet out."

She kicked Bliss on, urging the chestnut into the water. But her usually calm pony hesitated, rolling her eyes and dancing sideways.

"Bliss can feel the current pulling against her legs," Comet neighed worriedly.

"It must be even stronger where Lana is," Jess guessed. "She and Pie could get swept right out!"

Further out, Lana seemed frozen with terror as she clutched tight to Pie's neck.

"Hold on!" Ellen called to her. "I'll get help." She turned Bliss and rode her back onto the beach. "Does anyone have a cell phone? We have to call the coast guard!" she said in a shaky voice.

The other young riders shook their heads. "There might be a phone booth at the beach café," one of them said.

"There is no time to waste!" Comet whinnied. "Are you ready, Jess?"

"Go for it!" Jess told him in a low voice. "Don't worry, Ellen. We'll get the coast guard!" she said more loudly.

She felt a warm prickling sensation flowing down to the ends of her fingertips as bright violet sparks ignited in Comet's spotted coat and tiny rainbows flashed in his silky white mane and tail.

Something very strange was about to happen!

Chapter
FIVE

The magic pony gave a determined
snort and time seemed to stand still.

In what seemed like slow motion,
Comet leaped into the waves, trailing
invisible sparks like a shooting star. At the
same time, a thick mist settled over the
sea, hiding them from Ellen and the others
waiting on the shore.

"Hold on tight!" Comet warned Jess.

Jess gripped the reins as Comet galloped effortlessly through the deeper waves. Freezing water lapped against her, soaking her to the waist, but Comet's sparkly magic somehow kept her warm.

Lana's terrified pony was panicking. The thick mist seemed like another thing to be afraid of. With a shrill cry, the horse backed up and then spun around as it battled against the treacherous current.

"Hurry, Comet!" Jess urged. "Lana's barely hanging on!"

Comet opened his mouth and breathed out a whoosh of violet sparkles, which sprinkled around the other pony like fine rain. For a moment, Pie seemed to grow calmer. The pony stopped plunging into deeper water and stood waiting for Comet to reach it—until a particularly large wave washed the sparkles away.

Without Comet's calming magical influence, Pie kicked out strongly again. The current caught the pony and brought it surging straight at Comet and Jess. Jess gasped as Pie's flailing hooves seemed about to slam into Comet.

She didn't think twice. Leaning forward, she stretched out her arm.

Almost . . . almost. Yes!

"Got you!" Jess's fingers closed on Pie's wet mane and she managed to hold the

pony at arm's length, but then gasped
in pain as her arm twisted at an angle.
Gritting her teeth, she held on tight. "It's
okay, Lana. You're safe now!" she called to
the shivering little girl.

Lana didn't answer. She had her eyes
closed tightly and kept them shut, while
Comet towed her and Pie to shore. As
Comet splashed through the shallows
with Pie and Lana, every last bright spark
faded from his spotted coat. The thick
mist dissolved into strands and instantly
disappeared.

The moment they all reached solid
ground, Comet came to a halt. Jess finally
let go of Pie's wet mane, relieved to be
able to ease her aching arm.

Ellen had dismounted. She rushed
forward, grabbed the pony's bridle,

and then put her jacket around Lana's shoulders.

The other young riders cheered and clapped. "Way to go, Comet!" Ross yelled.

"Are you okay?" Ellen asked Lana worriedly.

Lana nodded. Her cheeks were now flushed and she seemed to enjoy being the center of attention. "It was really exciting! I wasn't scared at all!"

Ellen gave her a rather wobbly smile and then turned to Jess. "Thanks so much,

Jess. And thanks to you, too, Comet," she said, patting his neck.

"You are welcome," Comet neighed, but of course Ellen heard only normal pony noises.

"I feel awful. I should have kept a closer eye on everyone," Ellen said guiltily.

"You couldn't have known that boat would blow across the beach and scare Pie." Jess comforted her. "Anyway, no one's been hurt."

Ellen nodded. "I guess not. Hopefully Mom will be able to smooth things over with Lana's parents. We can't afford to lose any more customers." She paused and looked thoughtful. "That freaky mist was odd, wasn't it? It seemed to come out of nowhere."

"Um . . . yeah. Strange. Anyway, glad we could help," Jess said. She suddenly

realized how late it must be. She needed
to get back to the circus before she was
missed. The last thing she wanted was
for someone to launch a full-scale search
party! "I've gotta go now! Maybe I'll see
you here again?"

"Definitely. And come by and say
hello, if you're ever passing Bridgemore
Stables," Ellen said. "You can't miss us.
We're the first place you come to in the
town."

"Thanks. I will," Jess said, meaning
it. She'd love to meet up with Ellen
sometime.

She and Comet made their way back
along the beach. Now that the excitement
was over, Jess's injured arm began
throbbing. She winced at its soreness.

"You hurt yourself when you stopped Lana's pony from kicking me," Comet neighed in concern. "Let me make you better. Get down for a moment, please."

Jess dismounted awkwardly, trying not to bump her bad arm. The magic pony turned his head and blew out a big warm breath that twinkled with thousands of tiny sparkling violet stars. There was a faint crackling sound as the glittery mist surrounded her arm and then sank into it and disappeared. The pain increased for a second and then melted away, just as if it were sand pouring out of a bucket.

"I feel fine now. Thanks, Comet."

He bent his head and gently nuzzled

her shoulder. She reached up and leaned against his warm cheek. "We didn't get a chance to go and look along the cliff path, did we? Next time we go out looking for Destiny, we'll do that. And maybe we'll check out Bridgemore Stables?"

Comet tossed his head in agreement.

Chapter
SIX

As evening fell, the fairground came to life. Colored lights flashed cheerfully, organ music rang out, and the delicious smells of toffee apples, cotton candy, and hamburgers rose in the air.

Jess loved this time of day, just before night fell. The place had a fairy-tale atmosphere.

From where she stood at the center

of the merry-go-round, she could see the
line of people growing outside the big top.
Inside, the performers would be ready for
the show. The troop of horses was perfectly
groomed, and the clowns were in their silly
costumes.

Her dad was helping people climb the
steps up to the merry-go-round and mount
the painted horses. Once all the customers
were ready, Mr. Starkling gave Jess the signal
to start and she pulled the lever.

The merry-go-round began to move,

slowly at first and then turning faster and faster, its shiny gilded carvings and small mirrors flashing in the bright lights. Jess smiled at the carousel horses prancing up and down on their poles as they whirled past in time to the organ music.

A mother and her small child sat astride Comet. The child was laughing and clapping his pudgy little hands with glee. The magic pony tossed his head and whinnied with enjoyment.

"This is fun!" he neighed.

Jess smiled to herself. It had taken her a while to get used to the fact that she was the only person who could see that Comet was a real, living, breathing pony. She wished she could talk to him now, but there was barely time between customers to whisper a quick word.

It was a busy couple of hours, and Jess was glad when Mai came to lend a hand. "How's it going?" her cousin asked, expertly leaping aboard the spinning ride and weaving her way toward Jess.

"Good. It's been nonstop so far," Jess replied.

"I noticed," Mai said, reaching out and patting Comet's smooth spotted wooden back. "This horse is suddenly very popular. Everyone seems to want to ride on it."

"Really?" Jess said innocently. "I wonder why?" *It looks like people somehow sense that Comet's special, without knowing why*, she thought.

"I'm going to grab some coffee, now that you're here, Mai. I'll be back in twenty minutes. Do you girls want anything?" Mr. Starkling asked.

"Not for me, thanks," Mai said brightly.

"I'm okay. I'll get a drink later," Jess said.

Both girls watched Jess's dad walk away. Mai turned back to Jess. "Where did you disappear to this morning? I looked for you after I finished cleaning up the grounds."

"I went to the beach," Jess said truthfully.

Mai raised her eyebrows. "By yourself?"

"Yeah. I . . . um, needed to take a walk."

Mai wrinkled her nose in amusement. "Walk? You're weird."

Jess laughed. "I met a girl named Ellen. She was leading some kids on ponies. Her mom owns a horse stable in Lower Treen. She was really nice. You'd like her. Maybe you'll meet her sometime."

Mai shrugged. "It hardly seems worth it," she commented. "We'll soon be packing

up and leaving, and we'll probably never come back here."

Jess felt a stab of sadness as she realized that her cousin was right. It didn't seem possible that their way of life may have to change forever. She was sure that a perfect summer site must be somewhere—it was just a matter of finding it.

Mai operated the merry-go-round controls as the ride came to an end. The carousel horses slid to a halt and Jess helped a small boy and girl and their grandma climb down. The rest of the customers drifted away.

Comet turned his head and gave a friendly blow that ruffled her dark hair. His deep violet eyes were glowing.

"You're doing great," she whispered to him, patting his silky neck.

When she looked up, she saw Mai watching. Her cousin shook her head slowly. "Now you're *talking* to that spotted horse! What is it with you?" Mai came over and peered closely at Comet.

Jess had to try really hard not to burst out laughing as her cousin waggled her fingers and made silly faces, while Comet blinked at her calmly and swished his silky tail.

Finally Mai got bored and wandered

down to sit on the wooden steps that led
up to the carousel horses. Jess sat next
to her.

There was no one waiting for the next
ride. They could take it easy while another
line gradually built up.

A group of four tough-looking
teenage boys appeared between the stalls,
kicking cans and laughing and nudging
each other. They narrowly missed
bumping into a man with a toddler. The
man spoke sharply to them, but the boys
only laughed in reply.

"Uh-oh," Jess groaned, sensing trouble
brewing.

"Oh great," Mai echoed, rolling her
eyes. "I saw those guys messing around
earlier. They would show up here,

just when Uncle Kit's gone for a break."

"Maybe they'll go away," Jess said
hopefully.

"Fat chance!" Mai sighed. "Look out!"

Jess just had time to duck as one of the
boys kicked a can toward the merry-go-
round. It missed her by a couple of inches
and clanged loudly against the carousel
horse beside her.

"You idiot! You almost hit me!" she
cried angrily.

The boys nudged each other and
swaggered over. One of them, with short
hair and a thin mean face under a navy
blue baseball cap, glared up at her. "Who
are you calling an idiot?" he sneered,
putting his hands on his hips.

Jess swallowed. "Who do you think?"

she said, hoping she sounded braver than she felt.

One of the other boys called out. "Are you going to let her speak to you like that, Liam?"

"Nah! 'Course not. She's going to make it up to me!" Liam turned to Jess with a challenging grin. "Give us a free ride!"

Mai stepped forward. She squared her shoulders. "You wish! Get lost, you guys! Before I lose my temper!"

"Who made you queen of the world?" Liam mocked.

The other boys laughed. They exchanged glances, and then all four of them rushed forward and clambered onto a horse each.

"Go on, then. Start up this hunk of junk!" Liam ordered.

Mai folded her arms, the color rising in her cheeks. Jess watched helplessly as the boys stood up and began leaping from horse to horse and swinging around the poles. Jess saw Liam preparing to jump onto Comet.

Her lips twitched. *Big mistake*, she thought. *Huge!*

Chapter
SEVEN

Jess watched as the boy landed on
Comet's back and began jumping up and
down. His sneakers made a slapping sound
against the painted wooden saddle.

Comet gave an angry neigh and
slowly turned his head to look at the boy,
but, of course, only Jess could see this.

Suddenly Comet's deep violet eyes
flashed with mischief, and rainbow

sparkles twinkled in his mane. He bunched
his hindquarters, kicked out strongly, and
gave a mighty buck.

"Argh!" Liam appeared to shoot high
into the air. He whizzed toward a trash can
about five feet away and landed backside
first, getting jammed in the butt with his
legs and arms sticking up and waving
helplessly. "Help! I'm stuck!" he cried.

His friends jumped down and ran over.
Grabbing his arms and legs, they pulled
him out.

"Are you okay, bro?" asked one of them.

"What did you do that for?" another asked.

Liam scrambled to his feet, looking red-faced and shaken. "I just felt like it, okay?" he bluffed, eyeing the carousel horses warily. "That dumb merry-go-round is kids' stuff, anyway. I'm going on the bumper cars," he decided, slouching away.

"Hey! Wait for us!" The others hurried to catch up with him.

Mai scratched her head as she watched them go. "I don't get it! What just happened?"

"Beats me," Jess said innocently, grinning at Comet. "I'm just glad they've gone. Oh, good. Here's Dad coming back. I'll go and get us a cold drink." She scooted off before Mai could ask her any more awkward questions.

A few days later, Jess and Comet were exploring the cliff path. Below them, the sandy bay was visible in a wide curve. Seagulls soared overhead.

There had been no sign of Destiny or any other ponies, and Comet was becoming more worried.

Jess stopped Comet near an area where the path widened. She took in the wide sky, the deep folds and grassy slopes, and the cliff with the Needle stretching out to sea. The cliff path snaked across the hills, leading into the valley and the town of Lower Treen.

"I hoped we might bump into Ellen

again," she said. "Maybe she took the
riders somewhere else today after that
scare in the sea. I hope she didn't get into
trouble with her mom or Lana's parents."

Comet's long white mane lifted in the
fresh sea breeze. "I would like to see her
and Bliss again," he whinnied.

"Me too," Jess said eagerly. "We're not
far from Bridgemore Stables. Want to go
there? We can keep a lookout for Destiny
on the way."

Comet snorted eagerly, pulling at his
bit and springing forward.

Jess moved in time with his powerful
strides, taking in big breaths of the clean,
salty air. She didn't think she'd ever get
used to the wonderful sensation of riding
the magic pony. There was no one else
around, and she loved the feeling of

freedom. It was as if she and Comet were totally alone in the whole wide world.

The cliff path gradually led downward, and slopes of green hillside rose up on either side of them. Comet's hooves clattered as he stepped out onto the track that led into the town.

Almost opposite, Jess spotted a large redbrick building set back from the road. Beside the gatepost there was a sign with a rearing horse and the words *Bridgemore Riding Stables*.

Jess turned Comet in through the gates and they went toward the yard. She could see Pie, Bliss, and some other ponies tethered outside. As they rode up, Ellen came out. She was holding a body brush and a currycomb.

The moment Ellen saw that the visitors were Jess and Comet, her face lit up. "Hi, you two! I'm so glad you came by."

"We've been exploring the cliffs," Jess told her, dismounting and holding Comet's bridle. "We thought we might see you taking another ride."

Ellen shook her head. "I wish," she sighed. "We've had more cancelations. In fact, we only have four bookings for the whole day. I said I'd groom the spare ponies while Mom took the customers out. I thought it might take her mind off things.

She's worried sick about trying to keep the riding school going."

"Oh, that's awful," Jess sympathized. She remembered Ellen telling her that a brand-new horse stable had opened up farther down the coast. It looked as if things could only get worse for Ellen and her mom. "Do you want a hand?" she offered. "I'm used to grooming the circus ponies."

Ellen nodded, cheering up a bit. "Okay. Thanks. It'll be more fun if we do it together."

Jess tied Comet up next to Bliss. The chestnut pony gave a neigh of welcome and snuffled Comet's spotted neck.

"Aw, look at those two. Aren't they sweet!" Ellen said. "Bliss's really taken with your spotted pony!"

Jess grinned. *Comet's irresistible, all right!* she thought adoringly.

She filled a bucket of water so Comet could have a drink, before starting work. For the next hour it was pony-pampering time. Jess picked out hooves, brushed ponies' coats, and combed out manes and tails. Soon all the ponies were shiny and clean.

"Phew!" Jess swept a strand of dark hair back from her sweaty forehead.

"Time for a drink and a snack! I think we've earned it," Ellen announced. She led Jess into the large farmhouse-style kitchen.

They sat at the wooden table with their cold drinks and bags of chips. Munching on her snack, Jess looked out the kitchen window. She could see the road that curved past open fields and then back to the coast. Sunlight glittered off the nearby sea. "What a beautiful view," she said admiringly.

Ellen nodded. "I love it here and I'd hate to move, but Mom says we might have to. She wants to improve the stables, so we can offer indoor lessons and stuff. So she's been trying to sell a field she owns just outside the town to get more money to be able to do it. But no one wants to buy it, because it's not good for building houses on."

"What a shame," Jess said. "Is it a big field?"

"Yeah, pretty big. You can see for yourself if you go back to the beach by the road, instead of across the cliffs. It's got a 'for sale' notice. Why?"

"Oh, just wondering," Jess said. She was starting to tingle with excitement, as an idea began forming in her mind.

Chapter
EIGHT

The phone rang as Jess was leaving
Ellen's kitchen for the stable yard.

"I'd better get that," Ellen said. "It
might be a booking. Won't be long! I'll
catch up to you."

Comet gave a whicker of welcome
when he saw Jess. His intelligent eyes
twinkled at her as she untied him. Jess
felt her heart lift in response. Having the

magic pony for her friend was the best
thing in the world.

Holding his bridle, Jess patted his
silky spotted neck. "Ellen's just told me
that her mom owns a large field. It got
me thinking. We need somewhere for
the circus for next year, and she needs
to make some money. Maybe we could
help each other. What do you think?" she
asked.

"Perhaps we should go and look at
the field," Comet snorted.

Jess nodded. "Just what I thought. We
can check it out on our way back!"

She glanced at her wristwatch,
surprised to see that it was already late in
the afternoon. It wouldn't be long before
the circus people began getting ready
for the evening session. But there was

enough time to look at the field—if they
hurried.

Ellen came striding toward them. She
was holding the cordless phone.

Jess took one look at the older girl's
face. "Problem?" she guessed.

"And then some," Ellen groaned. "That
was Mrs. Penrose. Her daughter, Kay, is one
of our regular riders. Apparently Kay was
wearing an expensive necklace yesterday

and somehow lost it during the ride. Mrs. Penrose is furious. She says Kay won't be coming here again, and she wants Mom to pay for a new necklace."

"Oh no," Jess sympathized. She couldn't believe that this was happening to Ellen and her mom on top of everything else. "But how come it's your fault, if Kay lost it? No one should wear an expensive necklace when they go riding."

"Try telling Mrs. Penrose that," Ellen said glumly, looking close to tears. "I saw Kay when she arrived. And I'm sure she wasn't wearing a necklace, or I would have asked her to leave it in one of the lockers for customers' valuables." She sighed as she lifted the phone, ready to punch in a number. "I'd better call Mom on her cell. She's not going to believe this."

Comet pricked his ears. "Please tell Ellen to wait, Jess," he neighed.

Jess blinked, wondering what he was up to. But she trusted her magical friend's judgment. "Ellen! Don't tell her yet!" she said quickly. "Can you wait until she gets back?"

Ellen lowered the phone, frowning. "I guess so. But if you're thinking of going to look for the necklace, I wouldn't bother. It'll be like trying to find a needle in about ten haystacks."

Jess grinned. She wished she could tell Ellen that she had a big advantage. Comet! "Trust me. Everything's going to be fine! I'll be back as soon as I can!" she said reassuringly.

Ellen didn't look convinced, but she nodded and managed a worried grin.

The moment they were out of sight of

the riding stable, Comet slipped behind
a tall hedge. Jess felt a familiar tingling
sensation flowing down to the ends of her
fingertips, and violet sparkles glinted in
the magic pony's spotted coat. They were
brighter than she'd ever seen them and
they formed into a whirling tube shape,
which flashed with tiny rainbow glints.

Comet leaped forward into the tube and stood there without moving. The tube shape rippled, moving backward past them. Jess saw blue skies and sunlight, then darkness and glinting stars. A rosy dawn flushed the magical tube with its glow and then it was daylight again and they were trotting along the cliff-top path.

A salty sea breeze ruffled Jess's dark hair and she could see the last strands of morning mist as they dissolved in the sun. "Wow! You've taken us back to yesterday! That's amazing!" Jess exclaimed.

"No one will see us, Jess. My magic has made us invisible," Comet told her.

In the distance, she saw the line of riders, with Ellen's mom out in front of them on Bliss. Jess recognized Lana, Ross,

and more young riders from the other day.
A pretty girl she hadn't seen before was
riding a black-and-white pony at the back
of the group.

"That must be Kay Penrose," she
guessed. "Let's get closer."

Comet put on a burst of speed. As
they approached Kay, Jess saw the girl slip
her hand inside the neck of her T-shirt.
She drew out a gold chain with a sparkly
heart on it.

"Stupid necklace! I wanted a pony
charm bracelet!" Kay grumbled. Making
sure that no one was looking, she threw
the necklace into the air.

It glittered in the sunlight as it headed
for the center of a thorny bush. Comet
moved with the speed of light, leaping
high into the air, and Jess reached out.

Her fingers touched the chain. Yes! She
caught the necklace and folded it into her
palm.

"Our work here is done," Comet
neighed triumphantly as his shining
hooves touched down onto the grass.
He wheeled and set off back toward the
town.

"You're the best, Comet!" Jess cried.

She was reaching forward to pat him when she felt him stiffen and slow down. He stopped and stood staring down at the grass. Jess looked down, too.

In front of them and stretching away across the cliff top was a faint line of softly glowing violet hoofprints.

"Destiny! She's been here!" Comet whinnied excitedly.

Jess felt a pang. Did that mean he was leaving, right now? "Are . . . are you going after her?" she asked, her pulse racing.

Comet shook his head. "No. The trail is cold. But it proves that Destiny was here yesterday," he said, his eyes shining with new hope. "When she is very close, I will be able to hear her hoofbeats. And then I may have to leave suddenly, without saying good-bye."

Jess chewed at her lip as she realized that she'd been secretly hoping that he would stay forever. "You could both stay here with me and hide as carousel horses," she suggested.

"I am afraid that is not possible. We must return to our family on Rainbow Mist Island. Do you understand that, Jess?" Comet neighed gently.

Jess nodded, feeling her throat tighten with tears. "I . . . I understand," she said quietly, forcing herself to smile. She decided to try not to think about Comet leaving and to enjoy every single moment spent with him.

Chapter NINE

The last magical violet sparkles faded as Jess and Comet emerged from the glittery tube, which had brought them back to the moment just after they'd left Ellen.

"Isn't magic wonderful?" Jess sang out happily. But it was more wonderful, by far, to have a magic pony all to herself!

Comet came out from behind the hedge and trotted toward Lower Treen.

"You're going the wrong way. The stable's back there," Jess cried.

"I thought you wanted to look at the field that Ellen's mother owns," Comet reminded her.

Jess nodded. "Oh yeah! Sorry. I was so busy thinking about taking the necklace back to Ellen that I almost forgot. What would I do without you?"

They reached the edge of the town, and Jess soon spotted the empty field with its "for sale" sign. It was within easy

distance of the shore and was as flat and large as their current site.

Altogether it seemed perfect.

"I bet the circus and fairground would easily fit on here! And there's room for our trailers and everything. Maybe our horses could stay at Bridgemore Stables, too," she reasoned. "Now all I have to do is tell Dad and my uncles. And they can talk to Ellen's mom." She felt a moment of doubt. "Do you think it will work? What if Uncle Felix still wants to leave the circus, and my dad agrees with him? Maybe it will take more of your magic?"

"Magic cannot fix everything," Comet told her gently. "You have done all you can. Now you must leave it to the grown-ups to decide what to do."

"You're right," Jess said, smiling at her

friend's wisdom. "Let's take the necklace to Ellen before we head back to the circus."

Comet nickered in agreement.

As the gateway to the riding stable came into view, Jess could see Ellen and her mom in the yard. They were helping untack ponies and lead them into the empty stalls. The young riders were all gone, and Jess guessed that their parents had picked them up. Hopefully she'd be able to slip the necklace to Ellen without her mom noticing.

She was just about to ride into the yard when a familiar voice called out.

"Jess? Thank goodness!" Mai called, emerging from the track opposite. "I've been up on the cliffs looking for you. Everyone's worried sick. You've been gone for a long time. What are you doing here? And how come you're riding that pony?"

Jess froze, her thoughts whirling. "The . . . um, horse stable wasn't that busy today," she said, thinking quickly. "So Ellen let me . . . um, borrow Comet. But never mind that now. I've got some great news. I think I've found a new summer site for the circus!"

Mai listened as Jess quickly explained her idea about the empty field. "It sounds as if it could be what we're looking for," she said eagerly, when Jess had finished.

"I think so, too. But I don't know if Dad and the uncles will go for it," Jess mused.

"Well, here's your chance to ask them!" Mai exclaimed.

A car zoomed to a stop, and Jess's dad and Uncle Oliver got out. Jess saw that her dad had a face like thunder. Her spirits sank into the ground.

"Oh no. I'm in so much trouble," she whispered to Comet.

Comet gave a soft, reassuring blow to show that he was on her side.

"Jess! Where on earth have you been? You know better than to go off without telling anyone," her dad cried. "It's a good thing Mai remembered you talking about these horse stables."

"Sorry, Dad," she said in a soft voice. "I didn't mean to be late. I lost track of time. But I've got something to tell you—"

"That can wait. Take that pony back, please," her dad interrupted firmly. "We're leaving, right now. You're grounded, young lady!"

Jess knew when her dad meant business. She sighed. Everything had suddenly gotten so complicated. She couldn't think what to say or do.

Comet decided for her. "Pretend to take me back, Jess. You still need to give the necklace to Ellen," he neighed, going toward the stable.

"Okay," Jess whispered to him glumly. She had no idea what was going to happen after that.

Behind them, she heard Mai talking. "Dad! Uncle Kit! You have to listen to Jess. It's really important . . ."

As Jess rode into the yard, Ellen looked up and smiled. The tack-room door was open, and Jess could see Ellen's mom inside.

Quickly dismounting, she fished the
necklace out of her pocket and held it out
to the older girl. "I found it on the cliffs,"
she told her quietly. "Kay threw it away,
because she really wanted a pony charm
bracelet."

Ellen gaped at her. "That's amazing!
Thanks a million, Jess. Now I can call Mrs.
Penrose with the good news, and Mom

doesn't need to know. But—how did you find out that Kay lost it on purpose?"

Oops! Jess gulped. She shouldn't have mentioned she knew that part. Ellen would never believe the truth. "I . . . um, can sometimes tell fortunes and stuff. It's a family thing!"

Ellen looked impressed and then a puzzled expression came over her face. "Who are those people by the gate? They're looking up here and pointing. Do you know them?"

"Yeah, that's my cousin, Mai, with her dad, my uncle Oliver. And the other man's my dad. They came looking for me because I'd been gone for so long." Just as she finished speaking, Jess heard a sound she'd both been hoping for and dreading.

The hollow sound of galloping hooves overhead.

She froze. Destiny! There was no mistake. Comet gave an eager whinny and set off toward the back of the stable block, following the magical hoofbeats that were getting louder and closer.

Jess rushed after him. "There's something I have to do! I'll be right back!" she called over her shoulder to Ellen.

As she rounded the building there was a flash, and a twinkling rainbow mist floated down around Comet. He stood there in his true form—a handsome spotted pony no longer, but a magnificent magic pony with a noble head and proudly arched neck. Sunshine gleamed on his cream coat, flowing golden mane and tail, and the gold-feathered wings springing from his shoulders.

"Comet!" Jess gasped. She had almost forgotten how beautiful he was. "Are . . . are you leaving right now?"

Comet's deep violet eyes softened with affection. "I must if I am to catch Destiny and take her home safely."

Jess's heart ached with sadness, but she knew she was going to have to be strong and let him go. "I hope you and Destiny get back to Rainbow Mist Island safely. I'll never forget you," she said, swallowing her tears.

Comet spread his magnificent wings. "I will not forget you, either. You have been a good friend. Farewell, Jess. Ride well and true," he said in a deep, musical voice.

Jess rushed forward, threw her arms

around his silky neck, and pressed her face
to his glowing warmth. Comet allowed
her to hug him one last time, and then he
slowly backed away.

There was a final flash of violet light
and a silent burst of rainbow sparks, which
sprinkled down around Jess in crystal
jewels that dissolved with a chiming sound
as they hit the ground.

Comet soared upward. He faded and
was gone.

Jess stood there, feeling empty.
She could hardly believe that this had
happened so fast.

Something glittered on the ground.
It was a single shimmering gold wing
feather. As Jess bent and picked it up, it
tingled against her palm before fading to
a cream color. She put it in her pocket,

knowing that she would treasure it always as a reminder of her wonderful magic friend and the adventure they'd shared.

After a moment, she took a deep breath and prepared to face what was waiting for her. Comet had been so brave and fearless, and remembering that gave her courage. She started walking around to the front of the stable and almost bumped into Mai and Ellen.

"Jess! There's wonderful news!" cried Mai. "Our dads think it's a great idea to use that field for the circus site."

"So does my mom!" Ellen said, her face glowing. "They've all gone into the house to figure out the details. Now we'll be able to extend the stables and offer all sorts of stuff, like indoor riding and maybe even bareback riding! Isn't it great?"

"And there's something else," Mai said.
"When the circus is on the new site, your
dad says you can have a pony of your own.
He'll even pay for it to live at the stable!"

Jess blinked in amazement. "But how
did you know I wanted one?"

Mai grinned at her. "Did you think I
didn't know why you kept talking to that
spotted carousel pony, when you thought
no one was looking? You've wanted a
pony for ages, haven't you?"

Jess felt a delighted smile rising up from somewhere deep inside her as she linked arms with Mai and Ellen. There were some amazing times ahead for all of them! And none of this would have been possible if a magic pony hadn't chosen her to be his friend.

Take care, Comet. Good luck, wherever you are. And give my love to Destiny! she whispered to herself.

About the
AUTHOR

Sue Bentley's books for children often include animals, fairies, and wildlife. She lives in Northampton, England, and enjoys reading, going to the movies, and watching the birds on the feeders outside her window. She loves horses, which she thinks are all completely magical. One of her favorite books is *Black Beauty*, which she must have read at least ten times. At school she was always getting scolded for daydreaming, but she now knows that she was storing up ideas for when she became a writer. Sue has met and owned many animals, but the wild creatures in her life hold a special place in her heart.

Don't miss these Magic Ponies books!

Don't miss these Magic Kitten books!

Don't miss these Magic Bunny books!

#1 Chocolate Wishes

#2 Vacation Dreams

#3 A Splash of Magic

#4 Classroom Capers

#5 Dancing Days

Don't miss these Magic Puppy books!